BEAST QUEST:

NANOOK THE SNOW MONSTER

Adam Blade

First published in Great Britain in
2007 by Orchard Books Ltd
This Large Print edition published
by BBC Audiobooks
by arrangement with
Orchard Books Ltd 2010

ISBN: 978 1405 663700

Beast Quest is a registered
trademark of
Working Partners Limited
Series created by
Working Partners Limited, London
Text copyright ©
Working Partners Limited 2007
Cover illustrations ©
David Wyatt 2007
Inside illustrations ©
Orchard Books 2007, courtesy of
Orchard Books Ltd

www.beastquest.co.uk

British Library Cataloguing in Publication Data available

Printed and bound in Great Britain by
CPI Antony Rowe, Chippenham and Eastbourne

With special thanks to Stephen Cole

*To Karen, for all she's done on
the Quest*

Welcome to the kingdom of Avantia. I am Aduro—a good wizard residing in the palace of King Hugo. You join us at a difficult time. Let me explain . . .

It is written in the Ancient Scripts that our peaceful kingdom shall one day be plunged into peril.

Now that time has come.

Under the evil spell of Malvel the Dark Wizard, six Beasts—fire dragon, sea serpent, mountain giant, horse-man, snow monster and flame bird—run wild and destroy the land they once protected.

Avantia is in great danger.

The Ancient Scripts also predict an unlikely hero. It is written that a boy shall take up the Quest to free the Beasts from the curse and save the kingdom.

We do not know who this boy is, only that his time has come . . .

We pray our young hero will have the

courage and the heart to take up the Quest. Will you join us as we wait and watch?

Avantia salutes you,

Aduro

PROLOGUE

Albin ran across the ice field towards the football, ignoring the painful stitch in his side. He willed his legs to work faster, faster . . .

His team were a goal down, and it was getting dark. Soon everyone would return to the nomads' camp for dinner and the game would be over. If only he could equalise . . .

He reached the ball just a second ahead of the goalkeeper and booted it wildly. It flew through the open goal in a shower of snow.

'Yes!' he yelled, and his team surrounded him, whooping with delight.

'Your turn to get the ball,' said the goalkeeper sulkily. He wasn't happy!

There was no net in the goalpost, and Albin had kicked the ball so hard that it had landed somewhere in the snow dunes behind the ice field.

'You'd better be careful,' said another boy. 'The elders say they've seen snow panthers in the dunes.'

'Of course I'll be careful,' Albin grinned.

He had lived in the icy north of Avantia all his life and knew the wintery white landscape like the back of his hand—the ice fields, the frozen sea and lake, the snow dunes, and the nomads' camp where he and his family lived. 'There's nothing to be scared of!' he thought.

He ran to the edge of the ice field and scrambled up a snowy dune. From the top there was nothing to see but the hard, white landscape stretching out into the distance, glimmering in the

4

evening light. Albin shielded his eyes against the glare of the setting sun, but he couldn't see the ball anywhere. In the distance he heard his friends shouting and laughing as they made their way back to the camp.

He skidded down the other side of the slope to a narrow icy path that wound between the snow dunes. There was the ball. But . . . it had been squashed flat. He looked at it, puzzled. What had happened to it?

Then he heard a different noise. A strange, high, tinkling sound—like a bell.

As Albin gazed down at the ball, a shadow passed over him. A huge shadow.

With a sudden feeling of dread, he looked up.

A towering creature, five times his size, stood over him, rocking from side to side on its huge hind legs. Its shaggy fur was thick and white. Blood-red eyes glared down at Albin, and huge, curving, ivory claws sliced the air. Drooling jaws snapped open, showing razor-sharp yellow fangs. The Beast wore a small brass bell on a chain about its neck, but the fur there had been clawed away to reveal raw pink flesh.

Albin was too scared even to scream. He tried to turn and run, but his legs had turned to jelly, and instead he slipped and fell on his back.

The monster stamped one massive paw down on the icy path.

The shockwave jarred every bone in Albin's body. Panic-stricken he scrabbled up, hurling himself at the side of the snow dune to get out of the Beast's way. The monster's claws swiped against his side, tearing through his thick clothes to the flesh beneath. Albin yelled with pain. He put a hand to his side and felt warm, sticky blood. Desperately he scrambled up the dune. If he could only get to the top, in sight of the camp, he might be safe . . .

CHAPTER ONE

THE NORTHERN QUEST BEGINS

'Of all the places our Beast Quest has taken us,' Tom said, 'this must be the most amazing!' He stood still and stared out at the icy wastes. They stretched into the distance as far as the eye could see, bright shimmering white under a sky of vivid blue. It was late afternoon and the sun was strong.

'It's very bleak,' Elenna said, shivering. 'But it is beautiful, too.' Her pet wolf Silver pressed up to her, his grey fur speckled with snowflakes and studded with tiny icicles. She hugged him, grateful for the warmth of his body against her legs.

'I'll check the map and see how much further we have to go,' Tom announced. He pulled the well-worn scroll that Wizard Aduro had given him from his pocket.

His stallion, Storm, stood like a coal-black shadow against the whiteness all around, and gave a soft whinny as Tom patted his neck. Tom and Elenna could not ride him on the ice fields. His hooves kept slipping on the snow and ice, so their journey had been slow.

'We're close to the northern-most edge of Avantia. We must be nearly at the end of the trail.' Tom pointed to the red glowing path on the map that showed them their route.

This was no ordinary map. It had magical powers, and had been given to Tom by Wizard Aduro, special adviser to the king. The map had already guided Tom and Elenna to four different places on their secret Quest to rid the kingdom of the deadly threat

of the Beasts!

All his life, Tom had heard stories of the Beasts, legendary creatures that dwelled in the deepest corners of the kingdom, protecting Avantia and helping it to prosper. When he was a small child, growing up with his aunt and uncle, he used to think they were fairy-tales. He'd certainly never *met* a Beast. But then he'd never laid eyes on his father Taladon, either.

Tom still wondered if he'd ever meet

his father, but at least he knew now that the Beasts were real. Malvel the Dark Wizard had enslaved them with an evil curse and was using them to spread terror and destruction across the land. One special person had to take on the Quest to free the Beasts and save the kingdom from ruin. King Hugo and Wizard Aduro had chosen Tom. He was determined not to let them down!

He had set off with only Storm, his sword and his shield for protection. But soon he had met Elenna and Silver, and they'd joined him on his Quest. Without them, Tom knew he would never have made it this far. Together they had freed four Beasts from Malvel's curse, and now they were in search of the fifth—Nanook the snow monster.

Many of the rare herbs used in Avantia's medicine grew only in the icy northern plains, but without Nanook's protection, the nomads that lived there could not grow or gather them. Slowly the kingdom was running out of medicine! Tom knew they had to find the snow monster and free her. 'While there's blood in my veins,' he thought, 'I will not give up.'

'We'd better get going,' said Elenna, studying the map over his shoulder. She pointed to a small cluster of tiny tents, which stood up from the parchment, quivering slightly in the breeze. 'It looks as if there is a nomads' camp nearby. Perhaps we can stay the night there. I'm so tired I could sleep standing up!'

'Me, too,' said Tom. 'Let's go!'

As they set off across the ice once more—Tom leading Storm by his bridle, Elenna and Silver following—a sharp gust of wind blew up suddenly, making them all shiver, even though they wore heavy clothing.

Tom quickened his step. 'Come on—the sooner we're somewhere dry and warm the better.'

Then Silver stopped and barked twice loudly.

Elenna crouched beside him. 'What's wrong, boy?' she asked.

Tom saw the wolf's eyes narrow. A growl was building in the back of his

throat. 'Perhaps he can sense
something,' he said. The wolf was often
the first to smell danger.

A stronger blast of wind whipped at
their clothes. This time it didn't die
down. Within minutes it was screaming
towards them, and tiny shards of snow
and ice stung their skin.

'Don't tell me there's a snowstorm building up,' Elenna yelled over the wind. 'A moment ago the skies were clear blue and sunny.'

'Not any more,' Tom shouted. Now the sky overhead was dark grey and wild with driving snow. 'We must keep going and reach that camp.'

15

But with the sun blotted out by snow and cloud, he suddenly realised they had no way of getting their bearings. The map was useless.

'I think it was this way,' said Tom, turning into the thick grey and white haze, trying not to panic. He could barely keep his eyes open for the stinging snow. 'Or was it the other way?'

'I'm not sure,' said Elenna, as the storm grew fiercer around them. 'But we'll have to find shelter quickly or we won't stand a chance in this blizzard!'

CHAPTER TWO

BURIED IN THE SNOW

Tom had faced many dangers on his Quest—he wasn't about to be defeated by a snowstorm! But already his feet, hands and face were turning numb. It wouldn't be long before the rest of his body went the same way.

He gripped Storm's bridle and led him on through the driving snow, crossing his fingers that it was the right direction. But he wasn't sure . . .

'I can't see a thing!' Elenna shouted.

19

'Hold on to Storm,' Tom yelled back, but the wind whisked the words from his mouth before they could be heard. Desperately he broke into a stumbling run—then gasped as he hit something solid.

'What is it?' Elenna screamed over the wind.

'I've led us into a snowdrift!' he cried in despair.

Then he sensed Silver push past his legs and start burrowing at the huge mound of snow.

Tom felt a surge of hope. 'Of course! We could dig—'

'—a snow cave!' finished Elenna. She threw herself to her knees and started to claw at the packed snow.

'Wait,' said Tom, swinging his shield from his back. Given to him by Wizard Aduro, it was a charmed shield, and every time he freed a Beast he gained a new magical power. Now that he had fought the fire dragon, the sea serpent, the mountain giant and the horse-man, it could protect him from fire, drowning or falling from great heights, and it could even give him extra speed.

20

But at this very moment he could use it as a shovel!

He began to dig into the snowdrift with the edge of the shield. Silver helped by scrabbling at the drift with his heavy paws, and Elenna pulled Tom's sword from his scabbard and started chopping at the hard snow further in. 'It'll need to be a big cave for all four of us!' she shouted.

'The work will help to keep us warm,' Tom yelled back, smashing his shield against the drift. 'But I don't see how we'll get Storm inside . . .'

Hearing his name, Storm plodded forward and used his front hooves to loosen the snow. Tom felt a rush of pride. The four of them had come so far together, but only because they worked as a team. They would get through this deadly blizzard!

At last they had carved enough space to form a cave that would protect them from the worst of the weather. Elenna and Silver stepped inside first.

'Come on, Storm,' Tom said to his horse. The stallion could only fit his front quarters inside, but that would

block the entrance and help keep out the gale. Tom covered Storm's back end with blankets, and guided the horse's head and front legs inside the cave. Then he sat down next to Elenna on the snow.

It was dark and cold. They hugged their knees to their chests and huddled together for warmth with Silver between them. Storm lay with his muzzle resting on Tom's shoulder, snorting softly.

Tom and Elenna looked at each

other.

'It's the best we can do,' Tom muttered.

They sat in uneasy silence, listening to the wind howling and screaming outside. Would the driving snow block the cave and trap them inside? They could only sit and wait . . .

Then, all of a sudden, it stopped.

The wind died down. A chink of sunshine peeped into the cave behind Storm.

'I don't believe it,' said Tom, patting

Storm on the neck, encouraging him to back out of the shelter.

The stallion shuffled backwards from the cave, then stood up outside and shook away the snowy blankets. Silver shot out into the sunshine behind him, barking happily. Tom helped Elenna up and they crawled out of the cave together.

The sky was clearing and becoming bluer all the time, and there was still plenty of strength in the afternoon sun.

'It's as if the bad weather just gave up and went away,' said Elenna, mystified.

'It must have been a freak storm,' Tom decided. 'Come on—the sooner we reach that nomads' camp the better. Maybe they'll know where we can find Nanook.'

Her face suddenly serious, Elenna pointed to the ground. 'Look, Tom— maybe Nanook will find us first!'

There in front of them was a giant footprint. It was bigger than any footprint Tom had ever seen before and the deep indentations in the snow clearly outlined pads and claws. It was

the footprint of a large creature. A *very* large creature.

Tom gazed out at the empty ice fields. At least—they *looked* empty.

But now he knew the snow monster was out there somewhere . . .

And they had to cross those ice fields to get to the camp.

CHAPTER THREE

ENCOUNTER ON THE ICE FIELDS

Tom, Elenna, Silver and Storm pressed on towards the nomads' camp, skidding and sliding across the ice fields and looking anxiously around them for signs of the snow monster. Shallow pools of melted water flared brightly as they caught the rays of the evening sun. Tom wondered what was beneath the ice fields. Was it solid land? Or the

27

sea? There was no way of telling. They just had to keep moving on and hope for the best.

Then Tom spotted a dark speck moving towards them in the distance. He shielded his eyes and squinted. It was getting larger.

'Look!' he called to Elenna. 'We've got company!'

'What is it?' she said.

They both stopped and strained their eyes towards the speck.

As it drew nearer they could see it was a wooden sleigh, speeding towards them over the ice. It was drawn by a handsome golden pony.

A man sat at the front of the sleigh, wrapped warmly in animal skins and a fur hat. He was steering the horse with a long set of reins. 'Whoa,' he called out, and the golden pony obediently came to a halt right next to Tom and Elenna, his hooves perfectly at home on the ice. 'Greetings,' the man said. 'I am Brendan, chief of my nomad clan.'

Tom held out his hand. 'I'm Tom and this is Elenna.'

'Our friends here are Silver and

Storm,' Elenna added. 'Silver is a tame wolf. He won't harm you.'

'I'm glad to hear it!' said Brendan. He gently closed Tom's hand into a fist, then knocked his own against it. 'The greeting of my people,' he explained, then did the same to Elenna. He continued, 'It is unusual to find anyone travelling in the northern ice fields. Especially with such a fine horse.'

Tom hesitated. He supposed they must look suspicious. But the king had made him swear to keep the Beast Quest a secret. What was he going to say?

'Storm was given to me,' he said carefully, trying to avoid giving any details. 'I've ridden him halfway across the kingdom on an important mission.'

'Oh?' said Brendan. 'And what would that be?'

'Herbs,' Elenna blurted. 'We have come here to search for a rare herb to help treat a sickness that has swept through our town.' Tom saw she had crossed her fingers behind her back. 'The northern plains are known for

30

their herbal medicines, aren't they?'

Brendan nodded. 'Indeed. Perhaps we have the herb you seek. Arctic herbs are prized because they are scarce.' He crouched down beside a small patch of green leaves and carefully pulled them up. The roots of the plant were white and straggly. 'For instance, this is a kind of seaweed able to grow in ice. It helps to stop fever. We have built a camp here on the sea coast so that we can harvest it.'

'So . . . we've been walking over frozen sea?' Tom said anxiously, gazing at the ice beneath him. It had looked completely solid to him.

'Yes. The ice fields are thick in places and thin in others. You are lucky to have made it here safely.' Brendan tucked the plant into a pouch tied round his waist.

'We know!' said Elenna. 'We've just had to dig a snow cave to escape from a blizzard.'

Brendan nodded. 'We have many freak snowstorms these days. And the sun has been stronger. The warmth has meant that wild animals prowl the land in greater numbers. My son was attacked by one yesterday.'

'And without Nanook to protect you,' Tom thought, 'wild animals must be a terrible threat.'

'The ice fields are not as safe as they used to be,' Brendan continued, as if he had read his mind. 'These are harsh times, and nature is restless.' He added, 'You are welcome to come back to our camp and rest there. It is just behind the ridge of snow dunes at the end of this ice field.'

'Thank you! We will,' said Tom.

'But I'm afraid I only have room for one of you on the sleigh,' the chief said.

'You go,' Tom told Elenna. 'Storm and I will follow the tracks of the sleigh back to the camp.'

Delighted to be offered her first ride on a real snow sleigh, Elenna didn't need telling twice. Grinning, she jumped aboard behind Brendan. Silver leapt up, too, and snuggled beside her.

Tom waved as the sleigh sped back to the nomads' camp. But as the sound of it grew fainter and the eerie silence crept back, Tom looked around him at

the vast icy plains.

Nature was restless. And so was the snow monster. It must be Nanook who was causing the weather chaos. What else could it be?

Overhead, the sky was darkening once more.

'I must find Nanook,' he told himself. 'If it's the last thing I do!'

CHAPTER FOUR

TERROR BY NIGHT

It was almost dark by the time Tom arrived at the nomads' camp. It was made up of a large group of tents, gathered in a circle around an enormous bonfire. Some of the tents were short and squat, others tapering and tall. It looked like a miniature city built from sticks and animal skins. As Tom approached the camp, he saw the people were also wrapped in furs and skins. Everyone was bustling about their business—playing football, cooking over the fire, sweeping snow from the tents, and sorting the precious arctic herbs, before rinsing them or drying them over the fire.

Elenna was waiting for Tom in borrowed clothes made from tough leather. Silver jumped up at him, barking a greeting.

'I can't remember when I last felt this warm and dry!' Elenna said, pressing a bundle into his arms. 'Here are some dry clothes for you, too.'

Tom turned to see Brendan approaching with a young boy.

'Welcome to our camp, Tom,' the chief said. 'This is my son, Albin.'

'Hello,' said the boy. 'Do you want to see my wounds?' He lifted his woollen tunic to reveal three deep gashes in his side. They looked painful.

'Ouch! How did you get those?' Tom asked.

'I was attacked by a snow monster in the snow dunes, but I escaped,' said Albin proudly.

Tom and Elenna looked at each other.

36

'A snow monster indeed!' said his father. 'Whatever animal it was, you were lucky not to be seriously hurt—or worse. How many times have I warned you about straying too far from the camp?' He cuffed his son gently over the head.

Albin grinned cheekily, but there was fear in his eyes.

'It *was* a snow monster,' he said quietly. 'And it wore a bell around its neck.'

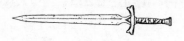

Soon the clan gathered round the campfire to eat, and Tom and Elenna joined them. But the mood around the fire was dark. Everyone was very quiet. Elenna fed Silver some of her stew and Storm was sheltering comfortably in the stables, where there was a thick bed of dried grass, as well as sweet-smelling hay and a bucket of water.

When night fell, they all curled up around the warmth of the flames to sleep.

Elenna and Silver were soon fast

asleep. Tom wished he could find rest so easily. Albin's encounter with the snow monster had done nothing to ease his fears at the thought of meeting Nanook . . . But he knew that it was his destiny to face up to these fears. His Quest was the most important thing he had ever done. Tom knew he couldn't give up now. Not when he, Elenna, Silver and Storm had come so far. They had to finish the Quest and save the kingdom!

Suddenly an unearthly howl sounded close by.

Silver woke instantly, his hackles rising and his teeth bared. Half-asleep, people scrambled to their feet in panic. Tom drew his sword, his heart pounding.

'It's a snow panther!' someone cried.

'It's right next to us!' yelled another. 'Run!'

'Don't move,' shouted Tom. Everyone froze. 'A panther might not attack us if we stay together,' he cried. 'But if we separate and try to run in different directions, it will go for whoever seems an easy target.'

The howl came again, even closer this time.

'Once Nanook would have scared off the snow panthers,' Elenna whispered. 'But now they're free to attack anyone whenever they want.'

Tom nodded. 'Thank goodness there's only one.'

But even as he spoke, Silver started growling again—at something in the opposite direction.

Elenna gasped. 'Tom—what if there's not just one! What if that snow panther's trying to distract our attention—'

'—while its friends creep up behind us!' Tom finished.

They spun round.

Sure enough, two sets of blazing green eyes appeared in the darkness beyond the fire.

'Watch out!' Tom cried.

With furious snarls, two enormous white cats bounded out of the night.

Instantly there was chaos. People were screaming, running in opposite directions, gathering children and shouting for their families.

He had to do something! Thinking quickly, Tom swung his sword into the bonfire and sliced through it, sending red-hot sticks, sparks and embers flying into the faces of the deadly animals.

The snow panthers yowled with pain and rage, and leapt backwards. But they hadn't finished yet. They were hungry, and could smell the remains of the stew around the fire! Screaming and screeching with anger, their claws extending, they bounded forward once more.

This time Tom snatched a flaming branch from the fire, waving it wildly towards the creatures and shouting at the top of his voice.

The panthers snapped their jaws, hissing like snakes, before giving up and slinking away into the darkness on their bellies.

'Thanks, Tom,' said Brendan grimly.

Tom drew a shaky breath, his legs trembling. 'It was Silver who saved us. Without him I wouldn't have spotted there were two panthers behind us.'

'The snow panthers have never dared come so near before,' a man exclaimed.

'What are we going to do?' a woman cried. 'Where can we go to find safety?'

Tom looked at Elenna. 'No one will ever be safe here,' he murmured. 'Not until we free Nanook to defend the ice fields again. We have to find that snow monster—and fast!'

CHAPTER FIVE

THE EXPEDITION

The next morning, Tom woke at dawn. The bonfire had died to a large mass of glowing embers.

He had a plan. But first he needed to borrow a sleigh.

He shook Elenna awake and silently they crept away from the fire, leaving the nomads sleeping. Silver padded quietly after them.

The chief had posted guards around the camp for the rest of the night, to watch out for any more snow panthers. The animals had stayed away, but their hungry howls had echoed throughout the night. Tom and Elenna found Brendan on guard at the edge of the camp, looking out towards the ice fields.

'We must leave the camp now,' Tom said. 'But we need a sleigh. Can you lend us one? We can't travel fast enough on foot, and our horse isn't used to the ice.'

Brendan looked at them sternly for a moment. 'Have you ever driven a sleigh?' he asked.

'No,' Tom admitted. 'But Storm and I make a good team. We'll soon learn.'

Brendan studied him closely. 'I think there is more to your mission than collecting herbs. Why else would you need such a fine horse, not to mention a shield and sword?'

Tom smiled awkwardly, but said nothing.

Brendan sighed and said reluctantly, 'I can see I shall have to trust you. All right then, come with me.'

He led Tom and Elenna to the

stables where they found a sturdy sleigh made from tree bark and skins. It ran on solid wooden runners.

Tom sat on the driver's seat, with Elenna and Silver settled behind him. Storm needed special ridged horseshoes to help him grip the ice, and held himself patiently while the clan's blacksmith nailed them to his hooves. Meanwhile Brendan explained how to steer a sleigh, showing Tom and Elenna how to pull on the reins with short, measured movements.

Once they were ready, Brendan guided the sleigh outside to the ice fields at the edge of the camp.

'Good luck, Tom and Elenna,' he said, then added, 'My son is convinced he saw a real snow monster. I had always heard that such Beasts protected the kingdom's people, rather than trying to destroy them. But there is a nameless danger that we talk of these days—the rumour is that it lies north of these ice fields, in a wide valley beyond the snow dunes.'

'Thank you,' Tom said, smiling.

'Be careful with my sleigh!' said the

chief.

'I will,' said Tom. Then he flicked the reins and shouted, 'Go, Storm!'

The stallion neighed, and a moment later the sleigh was moving north towards the ice fields.

Elenna waved goodbye, and Silver yapped joyfully. They were off!

Brendan raised his hand in farewell.

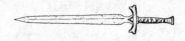

Tom slapped his reins against the front of the sleigh and gave a whoop of exhilaration. Storm picked up speed, responding swiftly to Tom's sure tugs on the reins. His ears flattened and his eyes narrowed against the icy wind, and he pulled the sleigh faster and faster, clouds of ice and snow spraying from his ridged horseshoes and the sleigh. Tom felt excitement surge through him as the sleigh bumped and careered over the uneven ground. The sun on the ice field was so bright it was blinding, and the cold bite of the wind whipped the blood into his cheeks.

46

They passed soft white bumps of snow dunes and jagged icy crevasses, glittering pools of water and rushing streams. There were dozens of places Nanook could be hiding, but Tom couldn't see any more telltale footprints or hear anything that sounded suspicious.

Soon the sleigh passed through a broad valley that rose and fell in great white sweeps.

'This must be the valley that Brendan told us about,' said Elenna.

All around them was flat white wilderness that seemed to stretch on for ever, surrounded by snow dunes on each side and interrupted only by clusters of spindly trees with wide, flat leaves. Tom noticed that the sleigh made a different, cleaner noise as it scraped along the ground.

'We must be on smoother ice,' he called back to Elenna. Remembering Brendan's warning, Tom wondered if this was thick or thin ice. Were they travelling over solid ground—or a lake on the floor of the valley?

At the same time, Tom noticed how

warm he felt in the thick, fur-lined coat that Brendan had given him—even out here on the icy plains. That couldn't be right! How could there be a snowstorm one day, then a heatwave the next? What was happening to the weather?

'Phew! I'm boiling!' said Elenna, echoing his thoughts. She took off her fur-lined coat and threw it over the seat beside her.

Suddenly Tom heard a thick cracking sound. He looked down. There were pools of water beneath the runners of the sleigh.

Elenna had seen the same thing. 'Tom!' she shouted. 'I think the ice is melting!'

He caught a glimpse of glittering turquoise water that looked much deeper than a puddle. Then he realised

that the ice had split open and the water underneath them must be a lake—just as he had thought! He felt sweat spring out on the palms of his hands. The water was a beautiful colour, but he knew it was fatal. If the sleigh plunged into the freezing water, they would all die!

'Whoa, Storm,' Tom shouted, and the stallion slowed to a halt.

But as the horse stopped, the sleigh lurched suddenly to one side. Elenna screamed, and Storm gave an alarmed whinny as the ice started to break beneath his hooves.

Before Tom could do anything more, the sleigh rolled again—catapulting Elenna over the side and through the ice into the deadly water!

CHAPTER SIX

THE RESCUE

'Elenna!' yelled Tom.

With a feeling of panic, he saw that she had vanished beneath the ice. Silver howled and leapt from the sleigh, scrabbling at the hole Elenna had made in the ice.

But Tom realised she probably couldn't see the hole, and must be swimming under the ice, trying desperately to fight her way back up to the surface! In the freezing water, she would hardly be able to breathe. Time was already running out!

Trying not to make any sudden movements, Tom slid down from the sleigh and fell to his knees, hunting for the tiniest flash of movement under the fractured ice. Every second counted! How long could Elenna survive in the freezing water? How long could she hold her breath?

'Elenna!' he shouted again, sliding on his knees across the ice.

Just then a shadowy blue outline appeared beneath the ice, some

distance from the hole where Elenna had fallen into the water.

Tom leapt to his feet and pulled his sword from his side. Taking a huge breath, he struck the hilt against the ice with all his might. This had to work! But in despair he saw that the ice was thicker in this part and wouldn't break.

'*Come on!*' Tom shouted, and drove the hilt again towards the ice with all his strength. By now he could see Elenna's hands pressed up against the ice below him. She was going to drown unless he could get her out *right now*!

As the hilt of the sword smashed down, the ice shattered and Elenna reared out of the turquoise water, gasping for breath and already blue with cold.

'Grab hold of me!' Tom yelled. He reached for Elenna's hands but she was flailing about, splashing hard and trying to keep herself afloat. 'Don't panic, you'll use up your strength!'

But Elenna dipped under the brilliant blue-green water again. Tom thrust his arm into the hole, and cried out in pain. It was colder than anything he had ever experienced. In seconds he lost almost all feeling in his hand.

Then Elenna resurfaced once more. 'Help, Tom!' she gasped. But she was struggling only feebly now.

Tom knew that if she went down another time, she would not rise again. He could not fail her!

He lunged forward with his freezing arm, gritting his teeth against the bitter cold. After all, he only had his arm in the water—Elenna's whole body was submerged in the sub-zero temperature!

'Hook your arm round mine,' he said. 'I've got you.'

Shuddering violently in the water, Elenna managed to raise her arm, but her hold on him was very weak. Tom was starting to shiver, too. He knew he had to get her out—but his arm was so numb he couldn't move it.

Suddenly Tom felt a pressure on the backs of his legs. It was Silver. The wolf had the reins of the sleigh in his teeth, and was hooking them round his legs! At once, Tom understood what he was trying to do. Storm was going to pull them both to safety!

'Silver!' Tom cried, relief flooding through him. 'You clever wolf!'

He reached forward and tucked his free hand under Elenna's armpit.

He heard Silver bark twice, and then felt himself being hauled backwards. Together he and Storm were towing Elenna out of the hole in the ice!

Tensing his muscles, Tom managed to hold on to his friend, as Storm dragged them both off the fragile ice, then onto safer, thicker ice. His heart was thumping like a hammer in his

chest.

When Storm finally stopped, Tom scrambled to his feet and helped Elenna up. Together they stumbled back to the sleigh. Tom lifted Elenna into the backseat and covered her with her fur-lined coat. It was lucky she had thrown it off before she had fallen into

the water—it was the only warm, dry piece of clothing that they had!

'I'm f-f-fine,' chattered Elenna, trying to smile. Silver whined and snuggled up to her, adding his own warmth to the coat.

'It's curious,' thought Tom, 'but even though the water's freezing, the

temperature outside is still warm. Too warm.' Lifting his head, he peered up at the sun and the blue sky. This wasn't the right weather for the north of Avantia. What was going on?

Storm whinnied with concern, pressing his head against Tom's chest, and Tom rubbed his numb fingers against the stallion's black mane. There was a pounding in his head.

'It must be my racing pulse,' Tom thought.

Then he realised that the pounding was coming from somewhere else. It was a distant thumping sound—a regular, menacing rhythm—and the ice was trembling faintly beneath his feet.

Tom listened hard. After a while he heard a second sound—the far-away tinkling of a bell.

It put a chill into Tom's heart.

'Nanook,' he whispered.

CHAPTER SEVEN

TORN APART

His heartbeat quickening, Tom looked all round. The horizon was bumpy with distant snow dunes, but there was no snow monster in sight. Then Tom looked down at his feet and saw an intricate lacework of cracks spreading over the ice with every thump. He caught his breath as the hairline cracks began to surround him. Storm might have thought he'd dragged them to safer ice, but it wasn't safe any more!

Suddenly he remembered the old stories about Nanook from his childhood. His uncle had told him that she was able to shatter ice with just a stamp of her foot . . . Under Malvel's evil spell, Nanook could start a huge natural disaster! If the ice fields tore apart, then the trade route to Avantia could never be passed. Medical supplies across the kingdom would dry up. People would get sick and die! He had to do something!

'Can you feel that vibration?' he whispered to Elenna.

Elenna, still shivering violently in the sleigh, looked down at the maze of hairline cracks in the ice. She gave him a fearful look. 'It's Nanook, isn't it?'

'We have to find her,' said Tom, nodding slowly. 'My guess is she's hiding somewhere in the snow dunes over there.' He pointed to the dunes at the side of the valley.

The distant, sinister jangle of a bell came again. It seemed to slice through his senses, like no other bell he had ever heard.

Elenna stared out at the dunes.

'What is that?' she asked.

'Albin said the snow monster wore a bell around its neck,' Tom said. 'Maybe it's an enchanted bell—part of Malvel's curse.'

Did that bell have anything to do with the warm temperature? It might have been his imagination, but it seemed to be getting hotter every time he heard it.

Suddenly they heard an enormous thump, and a huge tremor tore through the thick ice. A large, jagged crack appeared. Storm snorted in fear, and Tom gasped as he was knocked to his knees.

'The ice field's breaking up!' shouted Tom. He scrambled up and started pulling at Storm's harness. 'We must free him from the sleigh,' he said urgently. 'If it falls through a gap in the ice, Storm will be pulled into the lake. He won't stand a chance!'

Despite her shivering, Elenna managed to jump from the sleigh to join him, and together they wrestled with the buckles of the harness. The ice beneath them creaked and groaned. It

sounded like the moan of an animal in pain—as though the ice itself were alive! Storm whinnied in terror.

Finally, Tom undid Storm's last buckle and the stallion broke free of the sleigh.

Quickly Tom grabbed his sword and shield from the sleigh, and jumped onto the stallion's back, pulling Elenna on behind him.

'Yah!' he shouted. They had to cross the lake of ice and get to the snow dunes before the crack in the ice became a river!

With Silver sprinting beside them, they flew across the ice, the brilliant turquoise line of water splitting wider and wider behind them. Storm had never galloped so fast. The wind whipped their cheeks and blew the breath from their lungs. Would they make it?

'Faster, Storm!' Tom urged. 'Faster! We must reach those snow dunes!'

He could see Silver ahead of them, already safely at the dunes. But just before the edge of the ice, the crack overtook them! They were now faced with a stream of turquoise water that grew wider by the second as Tom and Elenna looked on in terror.

But Storm didn't hesitate. Gathering himself, he bunched his muscles and leapt forward. Tom felt the air whistle past him. It was as if they were flying! He could hear Elenna screaming behind him and Silver howling, as Storm's front legs reached out—and landed safely the other side on the soft snow with just inches to spare! Storm skidded to a halt before the dunes, throwing up clouds of snow from his hooves.

Just as they landed, the ice gave a huge, ominous boom, and the crack opened as wide as a river, stretching in

either direction as far as the eye could see. The deadly turquoise water churned and bubbled. Tom and Elenna watched as Brendan's sleigh pitched and rolled, then disappeared beneath the ice, lost for ever.

They sat panting, staring at the river in the ice field. It had split the icy northern plains from the rest of Avantia. Now they *had* to succeed in their Quest—if Nanook had split the ice field then only she could make it whole again. Otherwise, the healing arctic herbs could never leave the northern shores again, and many people in the kingdom would die for lack of medicine.

Tom turned Storm towards the snow dunes. 'It's time we met face to face, Nanook,' he said. 'While there's blood in my veins, I'll end this!'

Just then they heard a terrifying roar, together with the piercing, sinister chime of the bell. This time it sounded very close.

'This is it!' thought Tom, fear and panic rising up from his stomach. 'It's time to meet another Beast!'

CHAPTER EIGHT

FURY IN THE ICE

'I have to face my fears!' Tom told himself. 'This Quest is too important. I cannot fail. The kingdom of Avantia is counting on me!'

Determinedly, he touched his heels to Storm's side, and, with Elenna clinging on behind him, they galloped towards the snow dune and found themselves at the head of a narrow path.

The Beast was standing right in front

of them.

She was bigger than any monster Tom had ever imagined. Her fur was white, her eyes redder than a blacksmith's fire and her ivory claws looked sharper than daggers. Her hideous face was scrunched up with anger and hate, and around her raw, welted neck hung a tiny bell on the end of a gold chain. It glowed with evil energy. Nanook pulled at the chain, trying to tear the bell free, then howled ferociously and stamped a paw on the ground. The whole snow dune shuddered.

Elenna gasped in horror.

Then Nanook spotted them. Giving another terrifying roar, she lunged forward, her ivory claws reaching for them . . .

Silver yelped and Storm reared, throwing Elenna and Tom to the ground as Nanook closed in, heading straight for Tom.

Just in time he dived aside, his shield held above him, as the Beast's claws ripped through the air. Nanook's claws wedged deep into the wood and wrenched the shield away, then she turned and threw it straight back at him. He ducked, and it whistled past him back onto the ice field.

He didn't stand a chance without it. But now he had to run back over the treacherous ice to get it!

He set off at a sprint, his lungs burning and his legs pumping, expecting to feel the Beast's claws slice through his skin at any moment. Just as he was almost within reach of the shield, he slipped on the ice. Helplessly, he skidded past the shield, grabbing it as he went, then crashed into another snow dune.

'Tom, look out!' Elenna yelled.

He turned to find Nanook lunging towards him for a second time. Again, he swung up his shield to protect himself. The snow monster's huge paw smashed into it with enough force to knock Tom halfway up the snow dune. He heard Storm whinny with fear, and underneath the Beast's roar, the persistent jangle of the enchanted bell. His shield arm burned with pain. With a pang of terror, Tom knew Nanook was only just getting started.

'Elenna, take Storm and Silver and get out of here!' he shouted quickly.

The Beast stamped a huge paw down on the ice and thrust her jaws towards Tom as he lay stunned on the dune.

But then, with a deep, splintering crack, the ice gave way beneath her! In an instant she vanished down through a narrow, jagged hole into the freezing depths, just as Elenna had done.

Dazed, Tom watched the water churn and bubble.

'Tom,' cried Elenna from across the ice. 'Draw your sword.'

Tom shook his head, trying to clear it. 'What?'

'When Nanook comes up for air—'

But as she spoke, the water exploded upwards in a freezing fountain and Nanook broke the surface with a triumphant roar—giving Tom a clear view of the chain at the back of her neck.

'Quickly, Tom!' cried Elenna, as the Beast began to haul herself out of the icy water, her back towards him.

Taking a deep breath, Tom pulled out his sword, dived forward on his stomach and slid across the ice like a seal. As he reached the Beast, he slipped the tip of the blade between the raw, patchy skin on her neck and the gold chain, and twisted as hard as he could.

He managed to bend one of the links, but the thick, golden chain wasn't going to break that easily.

He drove the blade of his sword deeper into the link and pulled again, with both hands on the hilt of his sword. He strained back as Nanook plunged back into the freezing water, trying to drag him in with her, and roaring with anger. Tom leant all his weight back, bracing his feet as hard as he could on the slippery ice. He mustn't be pulled into the water! That would be the end of him. He could see the link in the chain bending further and further . . .

'Please break!' he begged it.

Then, all of a sudden, to his joy, the chain exploded! The golden links vanished in a burst of bright blue light,

as if into thin air, and the tiny bell
dropped to the ground in front of him,
silenced for ever.

'Yes!' he shouted, thrusting his sword
into the air triumphantly.

Nanook sank back into the water
without another sound.

Tom waited tensely for her to
resurface, but the turquoise water that
had swallowed her remained still. Had

he freed the Beast? Perhaps he had killed her? Had he failed in his Quest after all?

Then the ice smashed open in a sparkling cascade and Nanook reappeared, pulling herself out of the water and shaking the drops from her thick white fur.

Her eyes were no longer red, but a glittering icy blue. For a long moment,

Tom and the Beast looked at each other. Then the snow monster shuffled softly towards him. Tom drew in his breath but all she did was press her cold, wet snout against his cheek, as if to say thank you.

Then, abruptly, Nanook turned on her heel. She leapt forward onto the ice field, her arms pumping and her feet striding across the ice with amazing speed. Raising one giant fist in farewell, she vanished behind a snow dune. She was gone. More than that, she was free!

Tom felt a flush of pride. Another magnificent Beast had been unchained from Malvel's evil spell. How lucky he was! He'd come face to face with the kingdom's most powerful creatures. Most other people thought the Beasts were nothing more than myths, but he had met *and* fought them—and he was saving the entire kingdom of Avantia at the same time!

Noticing the tiny bell at his feet, he picked it up thoughtfully. The hot sun had disappeared behind grey clouds, and he could feel the temperature starting to plummet. Perhaps he had been right, and part of Malvel's curse had been to make the northern lands too warm so that the ice fields melted.

Then Tom's thoughts turned quickly to Elenna. As the temperature had dropped, she must now be feeling the cold from her dip in the icy lake. He ran towards her.

She was shivering violently on the snow dune, her teeth chattering so hard she couldn't speak, her skin blue with cold. Tom pulled off his own fur-lined coat and placed it round her, then held her close to share the warmth of his body.

'C-c-cold,' she said faintly, clutching his arm. 'But you freed Nanook!'

Silver licked her face and nuzzled her ear.

'*We* freed Nanook. We all did it,' said Tom. Then he added comfortingly, 'Don't worry. It'll be all right.' He tried to smile, but inside he was starting to panic. Elenna was soaked to the skin. Her wet clothes could be fatal in the deadly cold. Soon night would fall. Without shelter, protection or a sleigh to make their way back to camp . . . could Elenna survive until the morning?

CHAPTER NINE

THE HEALING

A loud whinny made Tom look up. Storm was standing at the top of the snow dune, staring out to the east, tossing his mane and stamping a hoof on the ground.

Tom had a feeling the stallion was trying to draw his attention to something.

'I'll be back in a moment,' Tom told Elenna, and quickly climbed up the dune.

From the top Tom could see down onto the vast ice fields. In the distance were two figures in a sleigh, which was drawn by a handsome gold pony . . .

Could it be Brendan and Albin?

'Hey!' he yelled. 'Help! Help!' But even as he shouted he knew that he was too far away. They would never hear him.

Tom threw his arms round Storm's neck. 'Stay with Elenna, boy. I'm going to get help!'

When he'd freed Tagus the horseman, Tom had been given a sliver of the Beast's horseshoe to put in his enchanted shield. That had given him the power of speed—and he needed it now!

Turning the shield upside-down, Tom jumped onto it and sledged down the steep side of the snow dune. But once he'd reached the bottom, he found he wasn't slowing down. In fact, he was picking up speed! The magic in the shield was working!

Soon he was racing on his shield across the ice field towards the sleigh. The wind was bitingly cold, especially

in just his woollen tunic, but he forced himself to concentrate on reaching the sleigh.

Then one of the figures stood up in the sleigh and waved wildly!

It was Albin!

'I thought you needed help!' he called.

Brendan smiled. 'He wouldn't let me rest until we came after you. He said he just had a feeling that you were in danger. Are you all right?'

Tom grinned with relief. 'We're fine—but Elenna needs your healing skills. You're not a minute too soon!'

'Did you see the snow monster?' Albin asked eagerly.

'Let's just say that your people are safe again,' said Tom, smiling. He had promised to keep the Quest a secret— he couldn't break that promise, even now that he had freed Nanook.

'I understand, Tom,' said Brendan, patting him on the shoulder. 'Thank you. The whole clan owes you a great deal.'

They quickly reached the valley where Elenna lay trembling. Brendan made her warm and comfortable with dry clothes and thick, woollen blankets, and his herbal treatments brought a rosy colour back to her cheeks in minutes.

'I told you it would be all right,' said Tom, squeezing his friend's cold hand.

She squeezed back and smiled. 'Thanks to you, it is!'

Brendan and Albin sped back to the camp to tell the rest of the clan that the northern lands were safe again—and to organise a great feast in celebration of the news!

Tom and Elenna followed on Storm, with Silver trotting alongside them.

'The ice fields that broke apart are joining back together,' Tom said.

'The land is healing itself,' Elenna agreed.

It was true. The wide turquoise river had already refrozen in parts.

They knew that with Nanook no longer breaking up the ice and the weather back to normal, the trading channel to deliver herbs and medicine to the rest of Avantia would be open. And Nanook would chase the snow panthers and other wild animals from the ice fields, so that the nomads could live and work in peace.

As they made their way through the snowy landscape they saw a familiar misty glow had appeared in mid-air. The glow slowly formed itself into the image of a white-haired man in a red cloak, who looked as if he was hovering on the ice beside them.

'Wizard Aduro!' Tom said. He knew the wizard was able to follow their progress from King Hugo's palace in the city. 'I wondered if you would come!'

'Once again you have acted bravely and fought well,' the wizard told them. 'Nanook is free to protect the northern people once again, and now the kingdom's medical supplies will get through to the rest of Avantia safely.'

'*Was* Malvel controlling the weather here?' Tom asked.

'His magic is strong,' said Aduro. 'He could influence the weather in a small area—through the enchanted bell around Nanook's neck. He could cause snowstorms or make the temperature rise. But when you cut it

loose, the spell was reversed.'

Tom pulled the tiny bell from his pocket. It seemed hard to believe that something so small could cause so much trouble.

'Place the bell on your shield,' the wizard instructed him, and Tom did as he asked. 'As the scale of the dragon protects you from fire, the serpent's tooth from water, the eagle's feather from falling, and the horseshoe fragment gives you speed, so the bell will protect you from extreme cold.' He looked at them gravely. 'But be warned. Magic alone is not strong enough to protect you from the fiercest Beast of all.'

Elenna shivered. 'Is that who we're meeting next?'

Aduro nodded. 'You must journey to the Far East, where Epos the flame bird awaits you. This will be your greatest trial.' The wizard glanced towards the nomads' camp. 'So first, you must rest. Eat and drink your fill. Build your strength for the long trek ahead—and for your battle with Epos.' He raised his hand in a salute, and his image began to fade from sight. 'Good luck . . .'

Then he was gone.

Storm whinnied quietly, and Silver looked up at Elenna.

'The fiercest beast of all,' Elenna echoed nervously.

'Let's not think about it tonight,' said Tom. 'Let's enjoy the feast and face the future tomorrow.'

New adventures were waiting. Was he strong enough to face them? Tom thought about his missing father. 'While there's blood in my veins, I will make him proud,' he swore. 'And I will follow this Quest to the end!'

BEAST QUEST:
NANOOK THE SNOW MONSTER